Just Like a Mama

WRITTEN BY
ALICE FAYE DUNCAN

ILLUSTRATED BY
CHARNELLE PINKNEY BARLOW

A DENENE MILLNER BOOK
Simon & Schuster Books for Young Readers
New York   London   Toronto   Sydney   New Delhi

SIMON & SCHUSTER BOOKS FOR YOUNG READERS
An imprint of Simon & Schuster Children's Publishing Division
1230 Avenue of the Americas, New York, New York 10020
Text copyright © 2020 by Alice Faye Duncan
Illustrations copyright © 2020 by Charnelle Barlow
SIMON & SCHUSTER BOOKS FOR YOUNG READERS
is a trademark of Simon & Schuster, Inc.
For information about special discounts for bulk purchases, please contact Simon & Schuster
Special Sales at 1-866-506-1949 or business@simonandschuster.com.
The Simon & Schuster Speakers Bureau can bring authors to your live event.
For more information or to book an event, contact the Simon & Schuster Speakers Bureau at
1-866-248-3049 or visit our website at www.simonspeakers.com.
The text for this book was set in Bembo.
The illustrations for this book were rendered in watercolor, gouache, colored pencil, and gel pen.
Manufactured in China
1019 SCP
First Edition
10 9 8 7 6 5 4 3 2 1
Library of Congress Cataloging-in-Publication Data
Names: Duncan, Alice Faye, author. | Pinkney-Barlow, Charnelle, illustrator.
Title: Just like a mama / Alice Faye Duncan ; illustrated by Charnelle Pinkney-Barlow.
Description: First edition. | New York : Simon & Schuster Books for Young Readers, [2020] |
Audience: Ages 4-8 | Audience: Grades K-1 | Summary: Carol Olivia Clementine wishes her
parents did not live so far away, but Mama Rose provides a home, loves her, and cares for her just
like a mother would.
Identifiers: LCCN 2019025752 (print) | LCCN 2019025753 (ebook) | ISBN 9781534461833
(hardcover) | ISBN 9781534461840 (ebook)
Subjects: CYAC: Mothers and daughters—Fiction. | Foster children—Fiction.
Classification: LCC PZ7.D72653 Jus 2020 (print) | LCC PZ7.D72653 (ebook) | DDC [E]—dc23
LC record available at https://lccn.loc.gov/2019025752
LC ebook record available at https://lccn.loc.gov/2019025753

For Mama and Pat
—A. F. D.

To my Mama Llama,
Sandra Leigh Pinkney
—C. P. B.

Mommy and Daddy live miles away.

I wish we lived together.

Maybe one day that will be.

I live with Mama Rose right now.
She is just like a mama to me.

Just like a mama, she combs my hair.

She buttons my winter coat.

And when I leave for school,
she waves and shouts
from her front porch,

"I love you, Lady Bug!"

Just like a mama, she teaches me things, like how to make my bed

and dribble
a basketball.

She bought me a watch when I turned five.
She taught me to tell time.

She bought me a bike when I turned six.
It is yellow like the sun.

In summer we ride
to the city park.
We listen to the
blackbirds sing.

Mama Rose tells me often,

"One day, child, when you grow up, you will spread your wings and fly."

My mother and father live far away.

I wish we lived together.

I wish that they were here.

But I live with Mama Rose right now.
She is just like a mama to me.

Just like a mama, she wrinkles her nose and calls my name when I don't eat my dinner.

"Carol Olivia Clementine! Green peas are good for you!"

"Yes, ma'am," I say.

I wrinkle my nose and
go ahead and eat 'em.
Because there will be
NO chocolate cake
until I eat my veggies.

Sometimes I forget to make my bed.

My bedroom is a mess and Mama Rose is not pleased.

Like a mama, she points upstairs and yells,

"Carol Olivia Clementine!
You have chores to do."

I run along. I clean my room. I know it is not perfect.

But I do my very best and Mama Rose sings my name.

"Carol Olivia Clementine!
You did a super job!"

My mother and father live far away.
I wish we lived together.
I wish that they were here.

I live with Mama Rose right now.
Mama Rose cares for me.

Mama Rose is a hug and a kiss.

Mama Rose is my home.

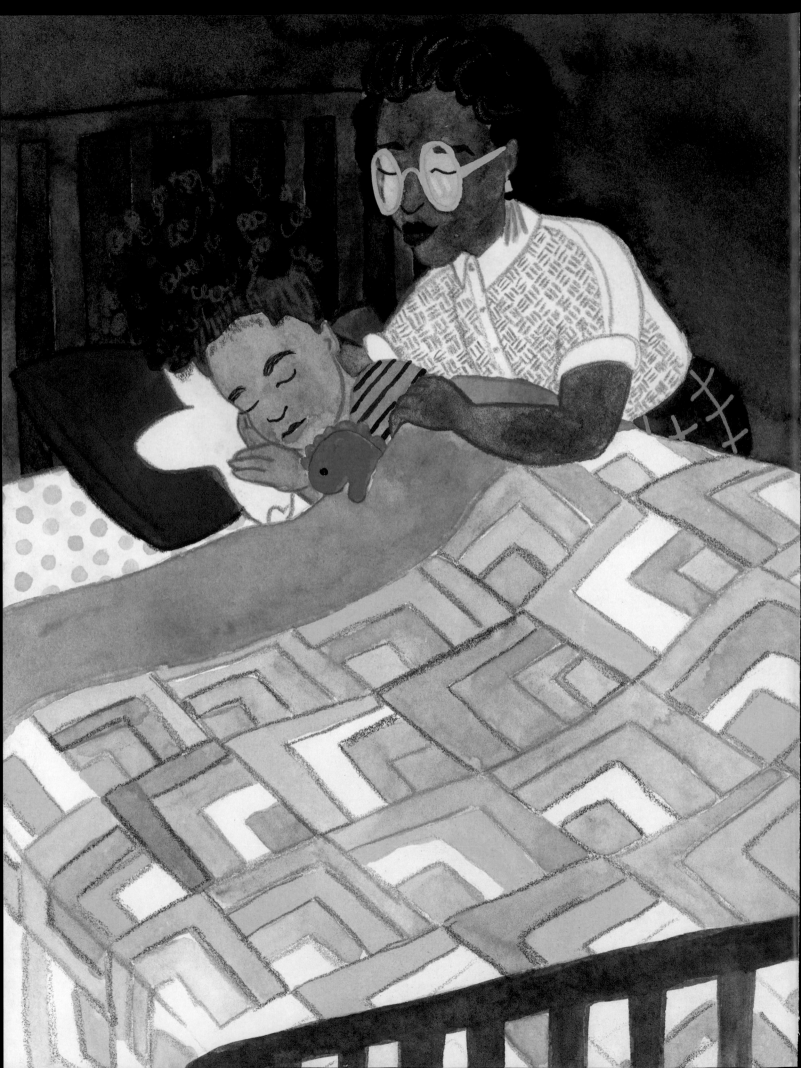

She loves me like a mama.

And I love . . . Mama Rose.

A Note from the Author

MY MAMA ACCEPTED a weighty task when my grandmother died in 1966. With her whole heart, Mama raised her baby sister, Pat, as her very own child.

Twelve years separate Aunt Pat and me. Mama has always loved us both with equal tenderness. Under her roof, she kept us fed, dressed us well, and sent both of us to college. Being the oldest one, Pat purchased music and gave me an appreciation for Stevie Wonder, Minnie Riperton, and the Brothers Johnson. When Mama wouldn't let me drive her car, it was always Pat who let me borrow hers. Aunt Pat is a big sister to me, and her sister is a mama to her. I believe it is love that defines our relationships. Blood related or not—love is the tie that binds.

When I was a college student in Dr. Elsa Barkley Brown's African American history class, she gave a lecture on slavery and "fictive kin." "Fictive kin" is a term that describes made-up or invented relations. Dr. Brown explained that the nefarious machinations of plantation life separated black families. In response to the separations, black men, women, and children formed chosen or voluntary kinships on the plantation to give their lives stability and meaning.

The process of choosing relatives and making families who are not related by blood or marriage remains a strategy of survival and well-being to this day. In these trying times, children are separated from parents for a myriad of reasons. The nation's social woes are too many to name. However, nurturing caregivers—whether compensated or unpaid, whether blood relatives, family friends, church members, or kindhearted strangers—are stepping up to be a safe haven for children in need of loving homes.

As a schoolteacher working in an urban environment with all of its complications, I have witnessed great success stories. I know countless grandmothers, aunts, and big sisters who did not retreat—who valiantly cared for children not their own until those children walked across a stage under shining lights to receive high school diplomas.

I wrote *Just Like a Mama* to acknowledge the efficacy of these relationships. I celebrate fictive kin, adoptive parents, and guardians who have chosen to love and care for a child when they have no obligation to do so. And as I offer readers my story, I dedicate the joy of it to Aunt Pat, Mama, and all loving families in every splendid form.